WELL READ!

GOOD WORK!

LET'S READ AGAIN!

I TRIED HARD!

LET'S PRACTICE!

HAVE FUN!

GOOD JOB!

HELP A FRIEND!

READING'S FUN!

LET'S READ AGAIN!

GOOD! WORD PERFECT!

BRILLIANT!

LET'S GO!

BE HELPFUL !

WELL DONE!

GOOD TRY!

WELL READ!

RIDE THE RAILS

I'M A TRAINTASTIC READER!

KT-161-974

EXCELLENT

WELL READ!

HONKING HORNS!

WELL READ!

TRY NEW THINGS!

LET'S HAVE FUN!

TAKE YOUR TIME!

IT'S TO GOOD SHARE

TRY YOUR BEST!

GREAT WORK!

GREAT READING!

GOOD EFFORT!

WORD PERFECT!

GOOD WORK!

First published by Parragon in 2009

Parragon
Queen Street House
4 Queen Street
Bath BA1 1HE, UK

www.chuggington.com

© Ludorum plc 2009

ISBN 978-1-4075-8009-8

Printed in China

BRAKING BREWSTER

Based on the episode "Braking Brewster,"
written by Sarah Ball.

Bath · New York · Singapore · Hong Kong · Cologne · Delhi · Melbourne

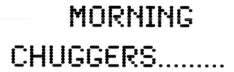

MORNING CHUGGERS.........

One morning, Vee had an exciting job for Brewster and Wilson.

"It's training time!" said Wilson, excitedly.

Brewster hoped they would be back in time to practice his new moves.

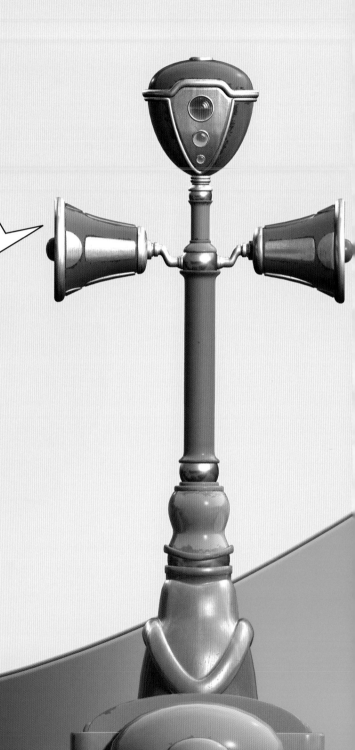

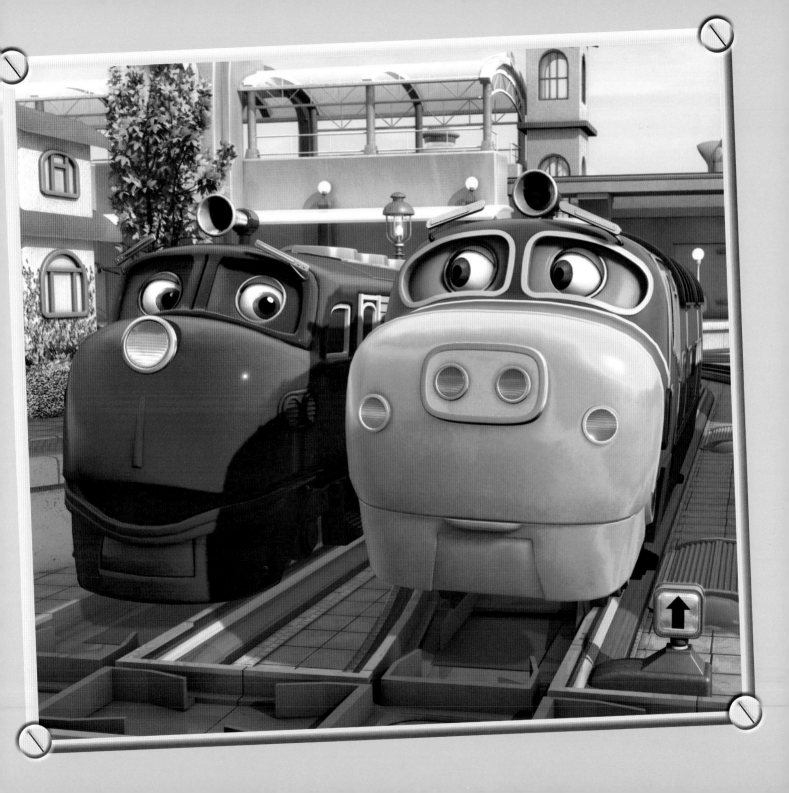

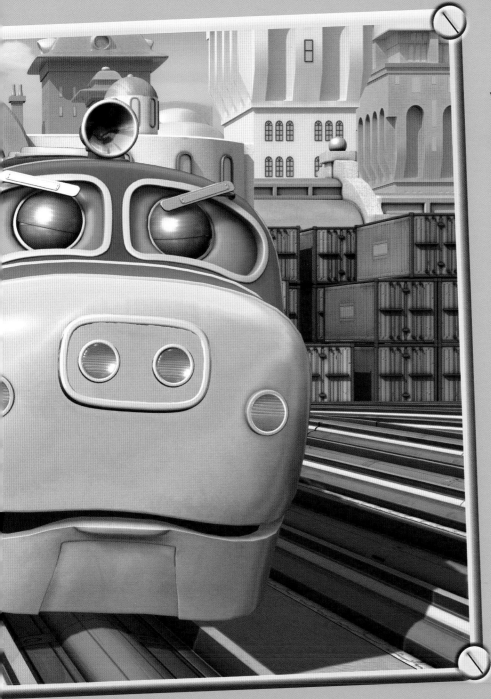

In the loading yard, Dunbar gave Brewster and Wilson hopper cars for training. He showed them what to do when they had a heavy load. "Doors...drop... load. Got it," said Brewster, confidently.

DOORS... DROP... LOAD!

Wilson found it really hard at first – but he kept trying. Then he did it!

"WAHAY"

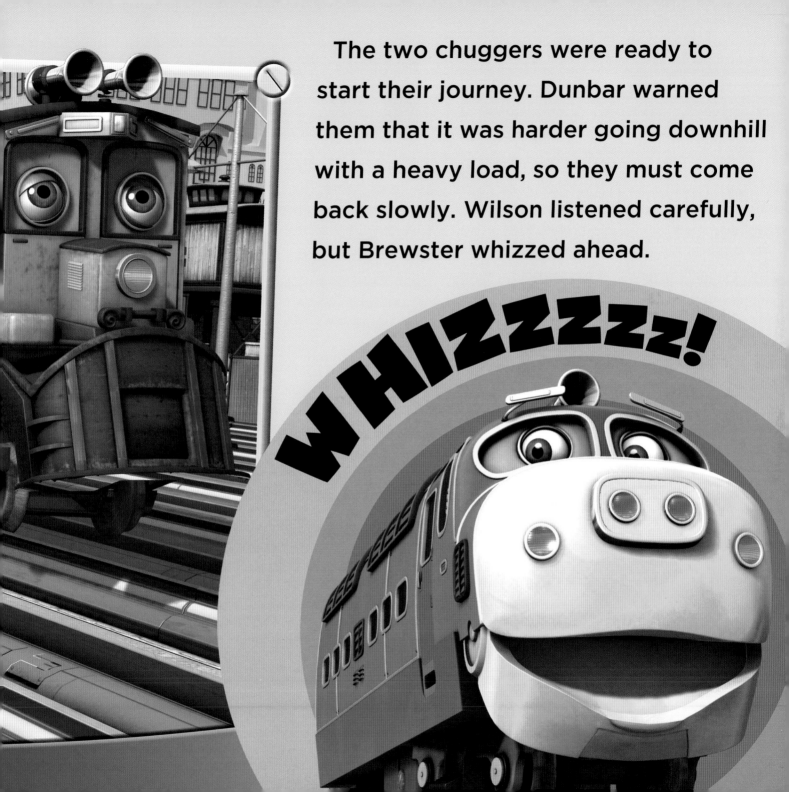

The two chuggers were ready to start their journey. Dunbar warned them that it was harder going downhill with a heavy load, so they must come back slowly. Wilson listened carefully, but Brewster whizzed ahead.

WHIZZZZz!

Vee told the chuggers to go to the mountain quarry to collect stone. They were to take the left tunnel at the mountain.

On the platform next to them, Morgan the mechanic suddenly slipped over on some oil. Wilson watched as Morgan sprinkled sand over the oil so his feet could grip.

"WHoOPS!"

When Brewster and Wilson
came out of the tunnel and
looked up at the mountain, they
saw it was a very long way away.

ZOOOOOOM!

They climbed the track, higher and higher up the mountain. Suddenly there were two tunnels in front of them.

Wilson couldn't remember what tunnel they had to take. He wished he'd listened more carefully to Vee, but he thought they needed the right one...

Before long, the tracks began to slope downwards. "Honking horns – we're going downhill!" said Brewster, worriedly.

They were going the wrong way! After turning around, they rushed back uphill and chose the tunnel on the left this time.

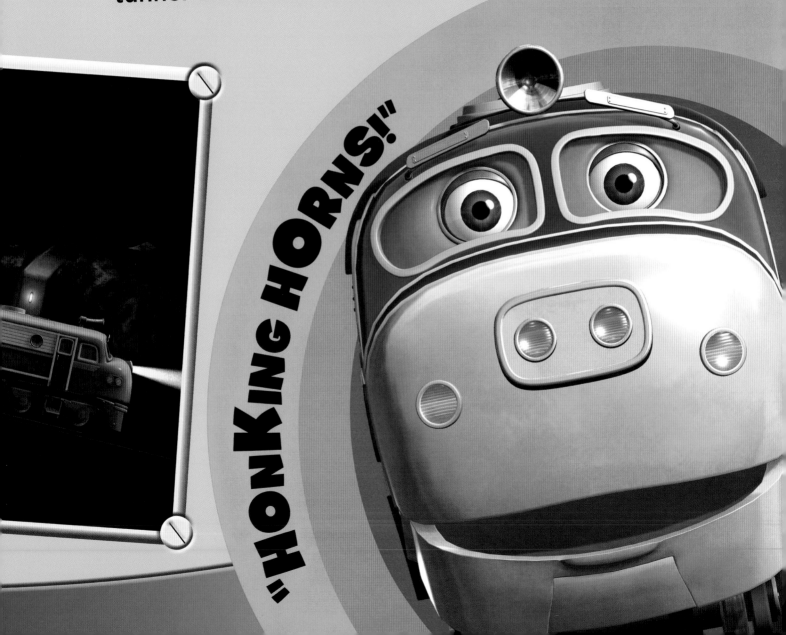

"HONKING HORNS!"

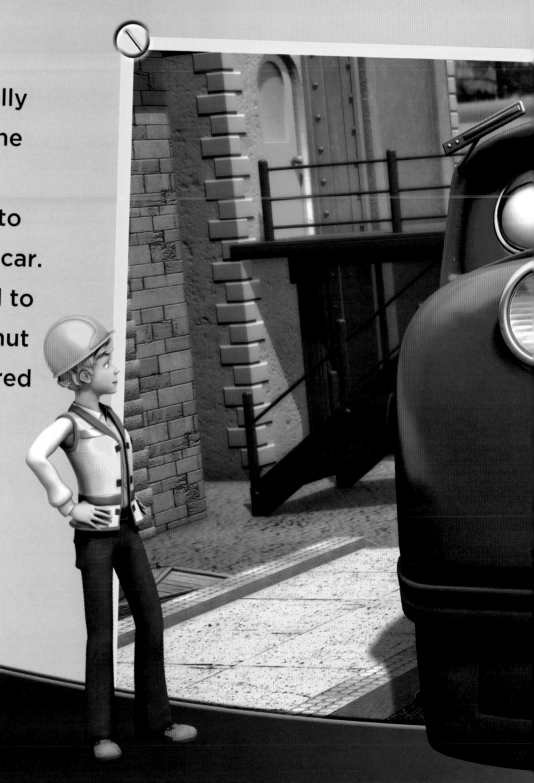

When they finally arrived, Karen, the quarry worker, loaded stones into Wilson's hopper car. Wilson struggled to keep his doors shut so Brewster offered to go first.

But when it was Wilson's turn, there was only dust left!

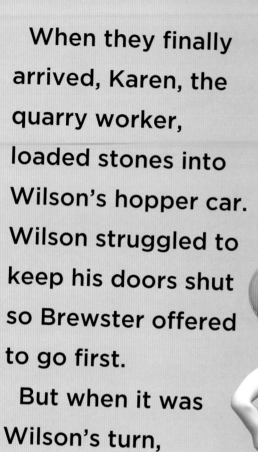

Brewster wanted to get back to the yard and zoomed ahead, but Wilson remembered Dunbar's warning – to be extra careful going downhill.

"Downhill's easy peasy," Brewster said.

Suddenly, the track became very steep and Brewster whizzed down the mountainside, out of control!
"My brakes don't work. Help! I can't grip the rails!" he cried.

"AAAAAAAAHHH!"

As Wilson caught up with Brewster, he had an idea. He whizzed ahead of Brewster and dropped his load of stone dust on the track.

"Brake on the dust!" Wilson called.

It worked!
They both slowed down
and came to a stop.
  "Thanks, Wilson, you
saved me," said Brewster,
very relieved. Wilson had
remembered that Morgan used
the sand to help grip when he
slipped on the oil.

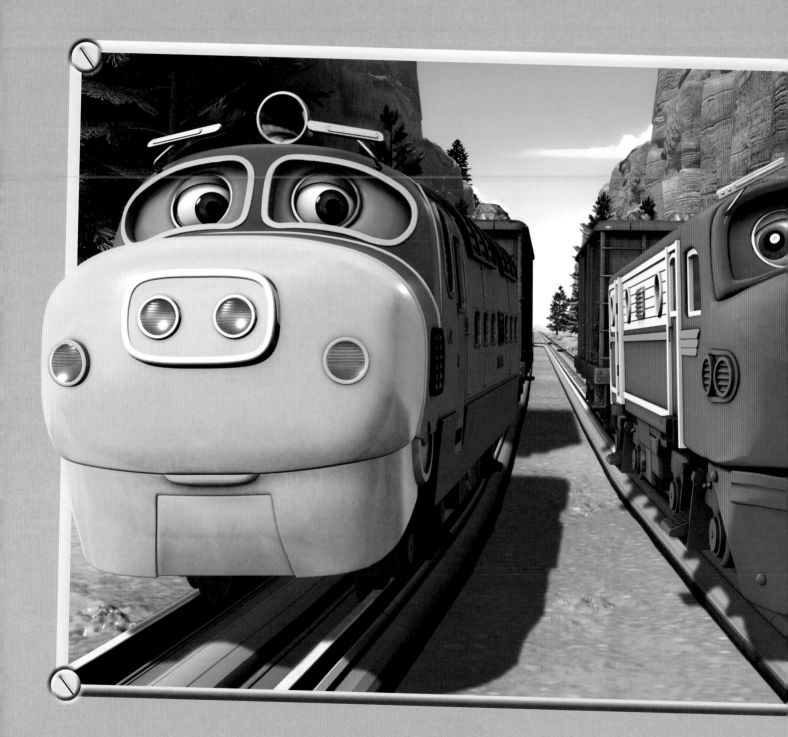

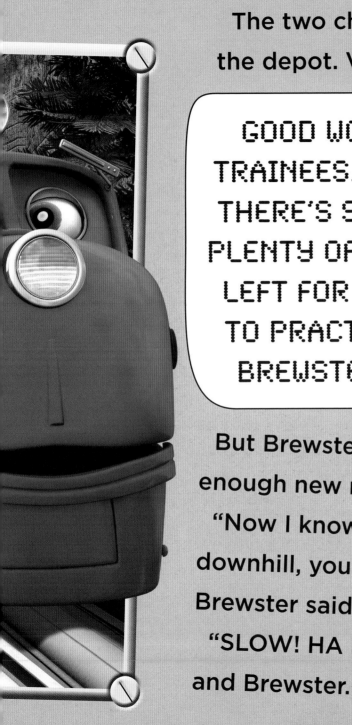

The two chuggers made their way back to the depot. Vee was pleased to see them.

GOOD WORK, TRAINEES. AND THERE'S STILL PLENTY OF TIME LEFT FOR YOU TO PRACTICE, BREWSTER.

But Brewster had tried out enough new moves for one day.

"Now I know...if you're going downhill, you have to go..." Brewster said, pausing.

"SLOW! HA HA!" giggled Wilson and Brewster.

Visit

www.chuggington.com

Now you can ride the rails with Wilson, Koko and Brewster!

Honk your horns! Here in Chuggington we need more little engines to join us and keep things ship-shape. That means you, trainee!

- ○ Paint your own engine
- ○ Meet the chuggers
- ○ Finish training tasks
- ○ Play games
- ○ Earn badges

Attention grown-ups!

Virtual Chuggington is a digital world where children can experience life from the same perspective as the engines. Think of it as a digital train set, one with an open-ended play pattern and storytelling capability that will awaken your child's sense of wonder!

Join us here, won't you? We can't wait to learn, work and play together!